Text and illustrations copyright © 2003 by Katie Boyce
Published by Bloomsbury, New York and London. Distributed to the trade by Holtzbrinck Publishers
Library of Congress Cataloging-in-Publication Data
Boyce, Katie.
Hector the Hermit Crab / by Katie Boyce. p. cm.
Summary: Hector, a shy hermit crab, is upset when flowers begin growing on his shell,
but he finds that they help him make friends.
ISBN 1-58234-800-6 (alk. paper)
[1. Self-confidence—Fiction. 2. Hermit crabs—Fiction. 3. Crabs—Fiction. 4. Friendship—Fiction.] I. Title.
PZ7.B691545 He 2003
(E)—dc21
2002026220

First U.S. Edition 2003
1 3 5 7 9 10 8 6 4 2
Bloomsbury USA Children's Books
175 Fifth Avenue
New York, New York 10010

In loving memory of my grandma,
Winifred Freda Boyce

HECTOR THE HERMIT CRAB

BY KATIE BOYCE

BLOOMSBURY

Beneath the
deep-green ocean
lived a hermit crab called

Hector.

Hector was very shy.

He would hide in his shell if another crab walked past, and he didn't talk to anyone.

One night while Hector

was sleeping, something terrible happened.

A flower grew on his shell.

"This is **terrible!**" he screamed when he woke up and saw it.

Hector tried **everything** to get rid of it.

He squashed and he poked, and chopped and sawed

More flowers were beginning
to grow and they
were getting **bigger** **B**

and

bigger

and

Hector was so tired and miserable after all his hard work that he went straight to bed.

To Hector's dismay, in the morning when he peeped out of his shell, he saw that a whole crowd had gathered around him. Hector tried to tiptoe off but the crowd followed him.

"Leave me alone!" Hector pleaded.

To his surprise the other crabs were actually very friendly

"We love your shell," they chorused.

"I wish I had a flower," said one.

"You look so pretty," said another.

Hector was delighted.

Soon he was chatting happily to the other crabs

and didn't feel quite as shy as he had before.

Making friends
wasn't so difficult
after all.